My ☆ Family ☆ ☆ C ☆

Oliver ☆ Moon

Dad →

Mam ↑

my Sister, the Witch Baby

Happy Birthday, Oliver Moon

Sue Mongredien

Illustrated by
Jan McCafferty

USBORNE

For all the children of Balfour Infant School,
with lots of love

First published in 2006 by Usborne Publishing Ltd., Usborne House,
83-85 Saffron Hill, London EC1N 8RT, England. www.usborne.com

A CIP catalogue record for this book is available from
the British Library.

UK ISBN 9780746086872 First published in America in 2010 AE.
American ISBN 9780794527600

JFMA JJASOND/11 01317/1

Printed in Guangdong, Dongguan, China.

Contents

Chapter One

"Twelve, thirteen, fourteen, fifteen…"
Oliver Moon said, counting the days on
the calendar that hung on the kitchen
wall. "Sixteen, seventeen, EIGHTEEN!
Only eighteen days until my birthday!"

It was early evening, and Oliver had
just got down from the kitchen table.
Oliver's dad was washing the dishes and

his mom was feeding the Witch Baby the last bit of her puréed slug pudding. Mrs. Moon smiled at Oliver. "Not long to go," she said. "You'll have to write out your party invitations soon."

"Ooh yes," Oliver said, thinking quickly. "Well, I'll invite Jake, of course,

and Colin, and Hattie, and Pippi,
and—"

"And ME!" the Witch Baby
interrupted, through a sluggy mouthful.

Oliver grinned at his sister. "Yes, you
may come too," he said. "Let's see, who
else…?"

"If you write me a list, I can send out some invitations by a Delivery spell tonight," Mrs. Moon said, scooping up the last spoonful of slug pudding and popping it into the Witch Baby's mouth. "Then we can start thinking about party games, and food, and—"

"Cake!" the Witch Baby prompted. "Me like cake."

"Me like cake too," Mr. Moon said. "What sort do you fancy this year, Ol?"

Oliver thought for a moment. He'd asked for a cockroach cake last year, but his dad had overcooked it, so that it had been more like a charcoal cake. Maybe a rat-tail upside-down cake decorated with fire ants? Or a frog-foot tart, with spider jam? "Umm…" he said, trying to decide.

Would it be very rude if he asked for a cake from the Magic Bakery on Cacklewick Street? They always had the most amazing

creations in their window. "Well, I was wondering—" he began, but his dad interrupted, looking excited.

"How about a big squishy worm cake with snake-juice icing?" Mr. Moon suggested. "I've always wanted to make one of those."

Oliver hesitated, then nodded. "Sounds great, Dad," he agreed. It was really nice of his dad to offer to make him a birthday cake in the first place, he reminded himself. And, besides, the Magic Bakery was very expensive – he would feel a bit guilty asking his parents to pay for a cake from there. "Thanks," he said. "Now to make my list for the invitations!"

Oliver went into the living room, and got some parchment and a quill from the cupboard. He sat down on the sofa, feeling excited at the thought of his birthday. He couldn't wait! After Christmas, it was definitely the best day of the year. His parents always brought him a special birthday breakfast in bed, then he got to open presents and cards with them, and then, at the party, he and his friends would play party games and eat lots of yummy party food. Even better, Oliver's birthday fell on a Saturday this year, too, so there would be no school. What luck!

Oliver started to make his list of who he wanted to invite: Jake, Hattie, Colin, Pippi, Mitch, Harvey, Lucy, Carly and Eric – they were all friends from his class at Magic School. Oh, and Granny Moon, of course. He definitely wanted her to come – she was always such fun at parties, as well as being one of Oliver's favorite people in the whole world.

He smiled to himself as he thought about what a great time they would all have together, away from the not-so-nice witches and wizards of Magic School. He certainly wasn't going to invite Bully

Bogeywort, his arch-enemy. Not likely!
Nor would he invite snobby Sukie
Swishcloak, sly Scott Shuffleslick or…
well, there were quite a few people Oliver
didn't like, actually. On a separate
piece of parchment, he wrote down the
names of all the people *not* to invite:

Bully, Sukie, Scott, mean Marcus Mudbreath and greedy George Gullet. *No way,* Oliver thought to himself with a shudder.

Then he jumped as a shout from his mom came through from the kitchen. "Oliver, I've just seen the clock! Get your pajamas on, please, it's past your bedtime!"

Oliver left his lists on the sofa and went upstairs to get changed. *Eighteen days and counting*, he thought to himself cheerfully. Oh, his birthday was going to be a good one this year, he knew it already!

"Have a lovely day at Magic School, dear," his mom said the next morning as Oliver put his cloak on, ready to go. "Oh, and I cast a spell to send out your invitations last night. Everyone should have got them first thing this morning."

"Thanks, Mom," Oliver said, opening the front door. He waved at his best friend Jake Frogfreckle, who was coming up the path. "Hi, Jake!" he called. "Did you get your invitation?"

Jake looked blank. "What?" he said.

Oliver walked down to meet him. "The invitation for my birthday party. Mom sent it last night."

Jake shook his head. "No," he replied.

"Oh," Oliver said. "That's weird. Well, it'll probably be waiting for you when you get home. Mom only said a minute ago that she'd sent them all out."

The two young wizards began walking
toward Magic School. They hadn't got
very far when they heard a familiar
voice. A familiar *horrible* voice. "Can't
wait for your party, Oliver!"

Oliver turned in surprise to see Bully
Bogeywort standing behind him, with

a smirk on his face as he waved a purple
envelope.

"What?" Oliver asked. "What do you
mean? You're not invited, Bully!"

Bully sneered. "Oh yes, I am," he gloated. "I got this invitation while I was having my breakfast, didn't I? Bully, you are invited to Oliver's party, it says. Saturday 25th, two o'clock."

Oliver stared at the purple invitation Bully was holding. And then he stared at Jake – who *hadn't* been sent one. *Oh, no*, he thought. Surely Mom hadn't sent invitations to the wrong list of people? Had she really invited all of Oliver's enemies, and none of his friends?

Chapter
Two

"I'm ever so sorry, dear," Mrs. Moon said helplessly that evening. "I saw the list and just worked the magic to invite everyone on there. I didn't realize you'd written *two* lists!"

"But you invited all the people I don't like!" Oliver groaned. "And I don't want any of them to come to my party!"

"Oh," Mrs. Moon said. "Oh dear. I *am* sorry, Oliver, I really am."

"Can't you do some kind of spell that…I don't know, takes the invitations back?" Oliver asked desperately. "Can't we say it was a mistake, and they're not invited after all?"

Mrs. Moon looked anxious. "That would be very rude," she replied. "And besides, their moms have already phoned to say they can come. All of them."

"All of them? What, Bully, Sukie, Scott, Marcus and George are ALL coming to my party?" Oliver cried in horror.

Mrs. Moon nodded. "I'm afraid so," she said. She put an arm around him. "Look, we can still invite your friends too.

It'll mean a bigger party than we'd planned for, but…"

Oliver's shoulders slumped. He couldn't believe it. "But Mom, Bully and that lot will wreck everything, I just know it," he groaned. "It will be the worst party ever!"

"Of course it won't!" Mrs. Moon said. "And no one will wreck anything. Nobody would be so mean as to spoil someone else's birthday party, would they?"

Oh yes, they would, thought Oliver, but he said nothing. What was the point? He already knew his party would be a disaster. A total and utter disaster!

The next few weeks went by very quickly. All of Oliver's friends replied to say they

could come to his party, but Granny Moon phoned to say she had been booked to speak at the High Wizarding Conference and didn't think she'd be able to get there in time. "I'm so sorry, Oliver," she had said. "I'll do my best to make it, but these things have a habit of dragging on very late, unfortunately."

Oliver was disappointed but

tried not to show it. Granny Moon was very famous in the wizarding world and had an extremely hectic life. She had been Mayor of Cloakley, the town where she lived, for eighty-seven years, as well as winning the gold medal in the Witching Olympics for her sorcery skills back when she was younger. It would have been great to have Granny at the party, especially as she could have helped keep an eye on Bully and the others – but Oliver knew just how busy she was.

In the meantime, he and his family were busy preparing for the party. They decorated the living room with black

and orange balloons and snaky party streamers, made goody bags for the guests to take home (with real pet tarantulas for everyone), decided on the games, and cooked lots of yummy party food.

"We'll have a great time," Mr. Moon declared, the night before Oliver's birthday. "You wait, Ol."

"I hope so, Dad," he replied, crossing his fingers. "I really hope so." He tried his best to smile, but he couldn't shake his nervous feelings. Bully had been going on and on at school about how much he was looking forward to the party, with a mean glint in his eye. And Oliver was *sure* he would try to cause trouble.

"Come in, come in!" cried Mrs. Moon the next day, as the party guests began arriving. "Hang up your cloaks, that's it, and go into the living room. We'll open the presents after cake, so if you could leave them on the coffee table, that would be perfect. Oliver! Your friends are here!"

"And your enemies," snorted Bully Bogeywort who was at the door. "Ha ha!"

"Gosh, what a teeny-weeny little house!" snobby Sukie Swishcloak exclaimed, wrinkling her nose in disdain as she thrust her cloak at Mrs. Moon and walked in. "Oliver, I didn't realize your family was quite so poor. Your whole house would fit into our kitchen, I think, don't you, Mommy?"

Oliver gaped in shock. He stared at Sukie's mom, hoping she'd reprimand Sukie for such a rude remark, but Mrs. Swishcloak merely gave a thin smile. "Now, now, Sukie, just because we are lucky enough to own a mansion, we mustn't tease those who aren't." She dumped her own cloak on Mrs. Moon, too, who was looking hurt at their comments. "I'll stay for a cup of nettle tea," she announced, as if she were speaking to a servant.

Oliver felt his fists clench with anger as they walked past, their noses in the air. How he wished Sukie hadn't been sent an invitation!

George Gullet waddled in next. "Where's the food? I'm starving," he said, his piggy little eyes looking all around.

"We'll be eating later," Mr. Moon said. "We're going to play some games first."

"Boring," George moaned. "I only came here for the food."

Mr. Moon looked a bit startled at this, but ushered George into the living room along with Jake and Pippi, who'd just arrived, and all the other guests. Mr. Moon clapped his hands together. "I think everyone's here now, which is great," he said. "So let's get this party started!"

Chapter
Three

"The first game is Pass the Potion," said
Mr. Moon. "Sit down in a circle, everyone,
that's it." He waited for a moment. "Er...
Bully? Marcus? Oliver's going to open
those later, okay?"

Oliver turned around to see Bully
and Marcus leaning over his pile of
presents on the coffee table, whispering.

They shuffled over to join the others at
Mr. Moon's words, looking somewhat
guilty at being interrupted. Oliver
couldn't help feeling suspicious. What
were they up to?

Everyone else was sitting waiting. Mrs. Swishcloak was the only parent staying for the party – probably because she wanted a good nosey around, Oliver thought to himself – and she perched gingerly on the sofa as if she were worried it might have germs.

Mr. Moon held up a goblet filled with a steaming purple potion. "While the music's playing, you have to pass this around the circle. When the music stops, you take a sip from the potion and see what happens."

"There are a few spells in there," Mrs. Moon added, with a smile. "Most of you will get a piece of cockroach chocolate or something yummy appearing in your mouth, but if you swallow a spell, you'll get a funny forfeit instead! Mind you just take a sip, though, okay?"

Mr. Moon waved his wand and party music started playing. He handed the goblet to Oliver. "Off we go!" he cried.

The goblet felt warm in Oliver's hands, and the potion smelled of blackcurrant and ginger. He passed it on to Jake who was next to him, then Jake passed the goblet on to Hattie. Along went the potion to Colin, Eric, Lucy…and then the music stopped.

"Drink, drink, drink!" everyone shouted at Lucy, who was holding the goblet.

Lucy sipped the potion and everyone fell silent, waiting to see what would happen. There was a flash of purple light…and suddenly Lucy turned into a small purple frog. "Croak, croak!" went the frog, jumping up and down next to Eric.

"It'll only last a minute," Mrs. Moon chuckled.

"Off we go again!" cried Mr. Moon, starting up the music. The goblet went round to Pippi, Bully, Scott...and the music stopped once more.

"Drink, drink, drink!" went the shout to Scott.

Scott took a sip…and beamed.
"Chocolate!" he said, with his mouth full.
"Yummy!" Then he sneakily took another
big gulp of the potion – obviously hoping
for more chocolate.

"Ooh, don't do that!" Mrs. Moon cried
– but it was too late. Everyone stared as
flashes of bright green sparkles crackled
all around Scott.

Then he turned blue in the face.

Then he grew very tall, zooming up higher and higher so that his head bumped the ceiling.

Then, in the blink of an eye, he turned into a little firework and whizzed all around the room, with golden sparks shooting from his ears. Finally, he fell to the ground, still tiny and firework-shaped, and didn't move.

Carly Catstail screamed. "Is he okay?"

"He'll be fine," Mrs. Moon said. "But I think he'll probably need a big sleep after all those spells." She picked up the tiny Scott, who was still rather blue around his mouth, and put him on a cushion.

"He's worn out after whizzing around," she said. "Shall we continue with the game? Make sure you only take a small sip, though, as I said. We don't want anyone else ending up like Scott, do we?"

Off they went for a third time, with the goblet being passed around the circle. The Witch Baby was so excited she got up and started dancing to the music – until mean Marcus Mudbreath knocked

her over with his elbow. He said it was
an accident, but Oliver wasn't so sure.
He glared at Marcus as the Witch Baby
burst into sobs.

"Can't someone shut that brat up?"
Bully muttered under his breath.

Luckily, the purple frog turned back
into Lucy at that moment, and the Witch

Baby stopped crying to stare with wide eyes. "Ooh! Frog gone!" she exclaimed. "Where frog gone?"

"Keep passing the goblet!" Mr. Moon reminded them. Around it went to George, Mitch, Harvey, Sukie…and then the music stopped.

Sukie rolled her eyes. "Do I have to?" she moaned. "It's a bit…babyish, that's all. I thought we were going to have magical entertainers here, not play silly baby games."

"Drink, drink, drink!" everyone chanted, Oliver loudest of all. He couldn't help hoping Sukie would get a forfeit. If only she could be changed into a frog for the rest of the party, that would be perfect!

Oliver watched as Sukie raised the

goblet. He was sitting quite near her and couldn't help noticing that as she lifted it, the potion suddenly turned a bright green and fizzed with little sparkles of light. *Wow*, he thought. Mom really had put some strong magic in there!

Sukie took a sip…and then let out the most tremendous burp.

"Sukie!" thundered her mother, choking on her tea. "Manners!"

"Sorry," Sukie said, burping again. "I can't…*burp!*…help it. It must be this…*burp!*…stupid potion!"

Everyone started laughing at the loud belches that kept coming from snobby Sukie. "Make it…*burp!*…stop!" cried Sukie to Mrs. Moon. "Please!"

Mrs. Moon shook her head. "I don't think it can be the potion," she said. "How peculiar! I didn't even put a burping spell in there."

Burp! went Sukie again. *Burp! Burp! Burp!*

When her daughter showed no signs of stopping, Mrs. Swishcloak got to her feet, looking disgusted. "Are you doing this on purpose?" she yelled. "You naughty girl – making a fool of yourself *and* me.

I'm taking you home this instant!"

"But Mom…*burp!*" Sukie cried. "I'm not…*burp!*…doing this on purpose!"

"Get your cloak," Mrs. Swishcloak barked. "I've never been so embarrassed in my life! Goodbye, Mr. and Mrs. Moon. I apologize for my daughter's dreadful manners!"

And with that, she was gone, dragging Sukie out behind her.

"Oh dear," said Mr. Moon.

"BURP!" giggled the Witch Baby.

"Always thought Sukie was full of wind," Jake chuckled, winking at Oliver.

Oliver couldn't help feeling secretly pleased that Sukie had gone home. He didn't like her snooty comments at all!

"Perhaps we'd better move on to another game," Mrs. Moon said. "I'm a bit worried about what else might be in that potion now. Who wants to play Pin the Tail on the Dragon?"

"Me! Me! Me!" came a chorus of excited voices.

"George? How about you?" Mr. Moon asked.

George Gullet had sneaked over to the
table at the side of the living room, which
was heaped high with party food. Oliver
saw him grab a few batwing chips before
he turned back to the others. "Just
coming," George said, crunching away.

"We're having the party food later," Mr. Moon said, rather pointedly.

"Yeah, whatever," George said, shrugging as if he didn't care.

Oliver bristled at George's rudeness toward his dad. With all the extra guests, there wasn't any food to spare. If George started pigging on it now, it would mean less for everyone else later!

"Bully? Do you want to go first?" Mrs. Moon called, in a rather sharp voice.

Oliver turned to see that Bully was over by the presents table again, fingering Oliver's gifts. Bully swung round guiltily at the question, his hands behind his back. "Yeah, sure," he replied after a moment.

Oliver stared at him as he walked past.

He couldn't be certain, but Bully's pocket did seem to be bulging with something. Surely Bully hadn't just stuffed one of his presents in there?

Oliver followed, casting suspicious glances at his enemy's pants' pockets the whole time. If Bully really had taken one of the presents, there was no way Oliver

would let him get away with it. No way
on earth! But how was he going to find
out the truth?

Chapter
Four

"Here comes the dragon!" Mrs. Moon sang out cheerfully just then, and Oliver was distracted by the picture of a large red dragon that magically appeared on the wall. Head, body, legs, tail…there was even a puff of smoke from its red nostrils that floated out into the room, making the Witch Baby sneeze in surprise.

Mr. Moon tapped on the dragon's tail with his wand, and it came away from the picture, scaly and red, just like a real dragon's tail. "Now for the blindfold," he said, waving his wand at Bully.

A thick black scarf appeared from out of nowhere and wound itself around Bully's head, covering his eyes so that he couldn't see.

"Ahh, you look much better now, Bully," Jake said cheekily.

Bully tried to swipe in the direction of Jake, but Jake dodged nimbly out of his reach. Mrs. Moon stepped in and took Bully by the shoulders, guiding him toward the dragon picture. She took Bully's hand and put it on the dragon's head. "That's the head, okay?" she said.

Mr. Moon put the dragon tail in Bully's other hand. "Stick it on the wall, son, where you think it should go," he instructed.

Bully groped around blindly, his meaty hands patting the wall as he thought about it. Then he stopped and put the tail in the middle of the dragon's back.

Everyone jumped as the dragon in the picture let out a roar of disapproval.

Bully leaped back from the picture as if he'd been bitten, scrabbling to untie the blindfold from around his face.

"Nice try, Bully," Mr. Moon said. "Who wants to have a turn next?"

Harvey had a go, then Mitch, then Eric. Just as everyone was giggling at the sight of the dragon with a tail sticking out of its nose, there came a high-pitched voice from behind them.

"Oh no! Here he comes again!"

"Help! Help!" squeaked another little voice. "Don't let him eat us!"

"He's grabbed six of us already!" came another squeal. "Stop him, stop him!"

Oliver and the others turned in surprise to see George Gullet at the table with his hand poised guiltily over a plate of cupcakes. "Oh, no you don't!" squeaked one of the cupcakes. "You greedy pig! He was at the birthday cake earlier, too, you know."

Oliver's eyes nearly fell out of his head. "Talking cupcakes?" he gasped, staring at them in amazement.

There was a bright green sparkly mist around the cupcakes, he noticed, and they all had little eyes and mouths. How come he hadn't noticed *them* before?

"Wow, how cool!" Hattie said, rushing forward. "I've never seen talking cupcakes before!"

"Neither have I," Mr. Moon said, looking puzzled. "And I *made* them! I wonder if I messed up the recipe somehow?"

Oliver stared at the green sparkly mist which swirled all around George, then vanished into the air. The same colored sparkles had swirled around the potion just before Sukie had sipped it, and before Scott had taken his huge gulp. At the time, Oliver had assumed the sparkles were something to do with the potion itself, so it was very odd that more of them had appeared around the cupcakes.

Mrs. Moon had gone over to the table and was looking sternly at George. "You haven't *really* eaten six of them already, have you?" she scolded. "We did tell you that the food was going to be for later — and there are only enough cupcakes for two each."

"And look at the birthday cake!" Eric cried out in horror.

Everyone stared. There was a big chunk missing from the squishy worm cake Mr. Moon had baked, and one of the candles was broken.

"Oh no!" Oliver cried, going over to see. "George! I can't believe you did that!"

George hung his head. He opened his mouth to speak but all that came out was an "Oink!"

"Oink is about right," Mrs. Moon said severely. "Now, come and join in like everyone else. And leave the food alone!"

George was looking horrified. He tried to speak again but all he could say was "Oink! Oink!"

"Come on, that's enough," Mr. Moon said. "Let's continue with the game."

Oliver's parents seemed annoyed with George, as if they thought he was messing around, but Oliver noticed that George's eyes looked as if they were brimming with tears. He was still hanging his head as if he were ashamed of himself, too. Oliver was sure George wasn't oinking on purpose. It was as if someone or something had cast a spell on him. But who?

Colin Cockroach won Pin the Tail on the Dragon. He was the only one to put the tail in exactly the right place — and as he did so, the blindfold whizzed off his head and the dragon burst right out of the picture. Everyone cheered in excitement as it flew all around the living room before swooping low to drop a prize into Colin's hands. "Wow!" Colin gasped, beaming down at the golden bouncy ball. "Thanks, dragon!"

"That was a great game," Pippi said, her eyes shining. "Really exciting!"

"Oh good," Mr. Moon said, smiling at her. "Well, the last game is a treasure hunt. Are you ready for the first clue?"

"Yeah!" everyone cheered. Well, *most* people, anyway. George could still only say "Oink!", and Bully and Marcus were both whispering again at the side of the room. Oliver strained to hear what they were saying, but it was impossible with all the excitement. *What's Bully up to now?* Oliver wondered. More present-stealing? Or worse?

"Okay, here's your first clue," Mr. Moon said. He unfolded a piece of paper and cleared his throat. "You heat up my bottom when you need to cook, peep over my side and have a good look."

"Heat up my bottom?" Lucy giggled. "What could *that* be?"

"A cauldron!" Hattie cried. "Where do you keep your cauldron, Oliver?"

"It's in the kitchen," Jake shouted. "This way!"

There was a mad dash out of the room.
Oliver gave a last desperate glance at
Bully and Marcus before Pippi grabbed
his hand and pulled him along. "Come
on, Oliver!" she cried.

Once in the kitchen,
they found a clue at
the bottom of the
cauldron which
sent them to the
bathroom. And
then, after
hunting around the
bathroom, they found
a clue under the sink
where the frog family
lived, which sent them
to Oliver's bedroom.

And there, under Oliver's pillow was a clue that sent everyone out to the garden.

Oliver was having so much fun, he'd almost forgotten about Bully and Marcus. It was only as they came back into the house that he heard his little sister's voice as she bossed someone around in the living room.

"No. Naughty! Not do that. No!"

The others were stampeding to find a clue near the front door but Oliver broke away to see what the Witch Baby was up to. He found her in the living room – with Bully and Marcus. She was very pink in the cheeks and seemed to be scolding them about something. "These for Ollie," she said firmly, stamping her little foot. "Not you."

Oliver's eyes widened as he saw what was in Bully's and Marcus's hands – his presents! There were hardly any presents left on the table. They must have already stolen the rest of them!

"Hey!" he cried, rushing into the room
– but before he could get there, Marcus
had given the Witch Baby a shove and
pushed her over. "Buzz off, shortie,"
he snarled.

The Witch Baby burst into howls and

Oliver ran over to her. "You leave her alone!" he yelled. "Pick on someone your own size!"

"What's going on?" Mr. Moon said, coming into the room. "Why aren't you joining in the treasure hunt?"

But before anyone could speak, a stream of green sparkles suddenly appeared around Marcus, and he began shrinking. They all stared as he grew smaller and smaller, shrinking down and down until he was about the size of a squirrel. "Hey!" he squeaked. "Turn me back again!"

"I didn't do anything," Oliver said, baffled. He stared all around the room, wondering where the green sparkles were coming from, but could see nothing.

"Nor did I," Mr. Moon said, coming closer.

The Witch Baby stopped crying and picked up the tiny Marcus. "You so cute!" she said wonderingly, prodding him in the belly. "You so teeny!"

"Put me down!" bellowed the tiny Marcus, but it came out no louder than a squeak.

"No," the Witch Baby replied, shaking her head. "Me play with you. You my *pet*!"

Oliver tried not to laugh at the look of horror on Marcus's face as the Witch

Baby started throwing him up in the air, giggling as she did so. "Wheeee!" she sang, chortling. "Wheeee, pet!"

Mr. Moon scratched his head. "There have been some very strange goings-on at this party," he said. "I can't understand it."

"No," Oliver said, in agreement.

He suddenly remembered what he thought he'd seen Bully and Marcus up to when he came into the room. He swung back to face Bully, who was looking as if butter wouldn't melt in his mouth — although he *was* wearing his cloak, which seemed to bulge at the pockets. Surely Bully hadn't been taking *more* of Oliver's presents?

"Bully," Oliver said, trying to keep his voice even, and not lose his temper. "Why are you wearing your cloak?"

Bully gave him a sneering look. "'Cause it's cold in here, of course," he replied, as if Oliver were stupid. "Why d'you think?"

"Why do I think you're wearing your

cloak?" Oliver echoed, glaring. "You really want to know?"

The treasure hunters burst into the room just then but stopped dead at the cold look on Oliver's face.

"Oliver!" Mr. Moon exclaimed. "That's no way to speak to your guest!"

Bully smirked, and something snapped inside Oliver. He'd had enough of Bully trying to wreck his party. He'd really had enough!

"I'll tell you why he's wearing his cloak," Oliver shouted, simmering with rage. "It's because he's stuffed a load of my presents inside it, that's why!"

Chapter Five

There was a shocked silence, broken only by Mrs. Moon bustling in, wearing an apron. "Time to eat!" she announced — then stopped, as she felt the tense atmosphere. "What's going on?" she asked. "Who won the treasure hunt?"

"Me, Mrs. Moon," Carly said meekly, showing a handful of golden biscuits.

"And... And Oliver just said Bully's been stealing his presents."

"Oliver said what?" Mrs. Moon cried in shock. "Oliver! Apologize at once! You can't speak to a guest like that!"

"Just what I told him," Mr. Moon put in crossly. "As if anyone would take your birthday presents!"

Oliver was just about to reply when the air in the room shimmered a strange green color…and then Granny Moon appeared!

"Granny!" Oliver cried, throwing his arms around her. "You made it!"

"I made it," Granny said, hugging him tightly. "In fact," she went on in a whisper, "I've been here a little while."

Oliver gaped at the sparkly green mist that clung to Granny's cloak. Did that mean…? Had it been *Granny Moon* making all those things happen to Sukie, George, Marcus and Scott? "Are you saying…?" he hissed.

"Just a bit of fun, I hope you don't mind," she whispered. "Now," she said in a louder voice, "did I hear someone mentioning something about food?"

"You did," Mr. Moon replied, smiling. "Hello, Mom," he said, going over and hugging her. "Have a seat. That goes for everyone else — come on, help yourselves!"

Nobody needed telling twice. There was a rush for the table, as everyone ran to sit down and start eating. There was also another twinkling of green sparkles, and Marcus grew back to his normal size, startling the Witch Baby, who'd been clutching him. "Sorry," he muttered to her as he sat down.

George, too, seemed to have had the

oinking spell taken off him. He went straight over to Oliver's parents and apologized for having eaten so much of the party food. "I'm really sorry," he said meekly. "It just all looked so delicious, I couldn't resist."

And there was Scott as well, looking dazed and still rather bluish as he sat down at the kitchen table.

Oliver sat down between Granny Moon and Jake, and started piling his plate full of goodies. There were sludge sandwiches, flea cookies, bowls of batwing chips and crunchy hairy caterpillars. The spoiled birthday cake sat forlornly in the middle, looking more like a ruined castle than a cake.

Meanwhile, Bully was still smirking at Oliver across the table, quite clearly thinking he'd got away with his present-stealing tricks. Oliver glared back. He was not going to let Bully leave the house with his presents. No way! But how could he stop him, after his parents had reprimanded him for even suggesting there was any wrongdoing?

"You look very thoughtful, dear,"

Granny commented. "Maybe I can cheer you up with this…"

She waved her wand in a complicated pattern, and pink and green sparkles fizzled at its tip. Then there was an enormous puff of blue smoke, and Oliver fanned it away with his hand, barely able to see. The smoke began to clear and Oliver blinked in astonishment. "Wow," he breathed. "Oh wow!"

His ruined-castle birthday cake had completely vanished and had been replaced by the most magnificent, spectacular birthday cake Oliver had ever seen – way better than anything from the Magic Bakery. It was absolutely enormous, with thick green icing, and decorated all over with curled rats' tails and slugs.

"Yummy!" the Witch Baby shrieked, banging on her high chair. "Me LOVE cake!"

"Oh, Granny!" Oliver exclaimed, hugging her again. "Thank you! That looks amazing!"

Granny Moon's eyes twinkled behind her glasses and she waved her wand again. This time, the room was plunged into darkness, and then lit candles and mini-sparklers appeared in the air, and floated down to stick themselves in the cake.

"Ooooohhh!" chorused Hattie, Pippi, Carly and Lucy in delight.

"Everyone ready to sing the Birthday Wizard song?" Granny asked, and led them all in chorus:

"*Birthday wizard, it's your day*

May all good magic come your way
We all wish you a splendid year
So clap your hands and give a cheer!
HOORAY!"

The mini-sparklers fizzled out and then Oliver leaned forward and blew out the candles. Everyone clapped and cheered, and the lights came back on.

"Make a wish, make a wish!" Hattie cried, smiling at Oliver.

"Yes, you must make a wish," Granny said, her eyes twinkling again. Then she gave a meaningful look toward Bully. "Think of something you really, really want…"

I wish I could have my presents back, Oliver thought at once, remembering his suspicions about Bully.

Green sparkly magic fizzled around the whole table, and then there was a whooshing noise as Bully Bogeywort suddenly shot into the air.

"He flying!" the Witch Baby marveled.

"Hey!" yelled Bully, looking frightened. "What's happening?"

Oliver and the others stared as Bully Bogeywort was turned upside down, as if an invisible hand were holding him by the ankles. And then gasps went up all around the table as presents – *Oliver's* presents! – began raining down from Bully's pockets onto the table.

"What the…?" Mr. Moon muttered in disbelief.

"Hey! Those are Oliver's!" Pippi cried,

outraged as she spotted the present she'd given him. "What were they doing in your pockets, Bully?"

"It was only a joke, I was going to give them back," Bully protested, but judging from the looks on everyone else's faces, nobody believed him.

"How could you do such a thing?" Mrs. Moon cried, looking horrified as one last present fell from Bully's trouser pocket and landed in the flea cookies.

Oliver glared at Bully. "I think you should go home," he told him.

"Yes, I will, I will," Bully wailed, starting to cry. "I'm sorry, all right?"

Granny Moon pointed her wand at Bully and magicked him away from the table. He fell to the floor with a thump, and ran for the front door, without a backward glance.

Granny Moon beamed at Oliver.
"Well, that's got rid of *him*," she said
lightly. "Now, should we try a bit of this
delicious-looking cake, do you think,
Oliver?"

Oliver smiled at his granny. His funny,
clever, brilliant granny. "I think that's a

very good idea," he said. "Would everyone like a piece of cake?"

"Yeah!" they all cheered.

Mr. Moon cut thick slices for everyone and passed them around. Oliver bit into the soft black sponge and felt happier than he had done all day. It had turned out to be a perfect party after all.

The End

Don't miss Oliver's fab website,
where you can find lots of fun, free stuff.
Log on now...

www.olivermoon.com

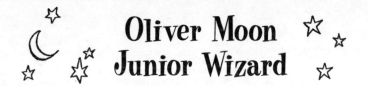

Oliver Moon
Junior Wizard

Collect all of Oliver Moon's magical adventures!